FRANK PERETTI
as Mr. Henry

Illustrated by Bill Ross

www.tommynelson.com

A Division of Thomas Nelson, Inc.
www.ThomasNelson.com

The adaptation of Reverend C. H. Woolston's "Jesus Loves the Little Children" is from #75 of the SEE and KNOW series by Mrs. Dan Whitaker.

Library of Congress Cataloging-in-Publication Data

Peretti, Frank E.
    Wild & wacky totally true Bible stories : all about helping others / Frank Peretti, as Mr. Henry ; illustrated by Bill Ross.
      p. cm.
    Summary: Humorous retellings of three Bible stories about helping others, each with an introduction and follow-up by "Mr. Henry," who relates the experiences of Biblical characters to modern life.
    ISBN 1-4003-0016-9 (hc)
    1. Helping behavior—Biblical teaching—Juvenile literature. 2. Bible stories, English. [1. Bible stories—N.T.] I. Title: Wild and wacky totally true Bible stories. II. Ross, Bill, 1956–   ill. III. Title.

BS680.S47 P47 2002
225.9'505—dc21

                                     2002033673

Printed in Colombia

03 04 05 06 07 QWQ 9 8 7 6 5 4 3 2 1

ALL ABOUT **HELPING OTHERS**

Ouchie, Mama! Oh. Hi, Mr. Henry here.

I think I've sprained my ankle. I should have fixed that loose board a long time ago.

Good thing I left my old medical bag where I can reach it. Let's see what I've got—Band-Aids, smelly goop . . . and lollipops! Looks like I can take care of my **boo-boo** until someone comes along to help me up.

I feel a little like the traveler from Jesus' story about a very helpful man . . .

One day, a teacher asked Jesus lots of questions about how to get into heaven. Jesus responded by asking the teacher what the law books said.

"Love the Lord God with all your heart, all your soul, all your strength, and all your mind," the teacher answered. "And they say, 'Love your neighbor as you love yourself.'"

"Well, there's your answer," Jesus commented.

"Wait," the teacher said. "I still don't get it. Who counts as my neighbor?"

To explain, Jesus told the teacher the story of the Good Samaritan.

A man once traveled down the road from Jerusalem to Jericho. Enjoying his outing, he whistled a happy tune as he walked. This traveler didn't notice two sneaky ROBBERS hiding in the bushes.

The robbers jumped into the road and tackled the traveler. Then they beat him up and ran away, leaving him on the side of the road.

A short while later, a priest zipped by. *I must get to the temple,* thought the **priest.** *Mounds of work to do . . . Temple bazaar to plan . . . Sermon to compose . . .*

But when he heard a long moan—"Ohhh-aagh"—he screeched to a stop. Then he saw the injured traveler.

Hmmm. That man sounds hurt. Wish I had time to help him. Maybe he won't notice me if I'm on the other side of the road.

The priest crossed the road and jogged away, covering his face. But God still saw him.

Soon, another worker from the temple scooted down the road.

As he walked, he prayed, "Oh, my dear Lord, my precious Lord, I want to be Your servant. Oh, I'm Yours, I'm Yours, I'm Yours. Yes, I want to help people and do good."

He tripped over the hurt traveler.

"Who left this man in the middle of the road? How rude . . . anyway, as I was saying, Lord, use me to help others."

And he continued down the road.

Before long, someone else came by.

"Whoa, Gertrude. Slow down," said the man from Samaria to his donkey. He had spotted the hurt traveler.

"May I help you, partner?" asked the Good **Samaritan.**

The traveler groaned and moaned and tried to whistle his happy tune.

Good Sammy grabbed his medical bag, cleaned the traveler's wounds, and put Band-Aids on them. Then he helped the traveler climb onto Gertrude, and they headed for town.

The Good Samaritan took the weary traveler to a five-star hotel with twenty-four-hour room service, cable TV, and fluffy white pillows.

Good Sammy said to the innkeeper, "Here's some **MONEY** for the traveler's room. And here's a little extra, in case he needs some curly fries or a double-fudge sundae. Take really good care of him. If he needs anything else, I'll pay for it when I return."

"So someone finally helped the traveler," finished Jesus. Then He asked, "Now which of those three—the priest, the righteous man, or the Samaritan—acted as a good **neighbor?**"

"Good Sammy, of course!" answered the teacher. "He stopped and helped. He was giving and loving and all that good stuff."

"That's right," said Jesus. "He loved another as he loved himself. Now, go out and try to love your neighbor just like the Samaritan did."

We must help others when we see their needs. We can't assume someone else will come along.

Slow down and make time to **HeLP,** even if you're in a hurry. God has given us each precious gifts. Don't take them for granted. Instead, use them to help others.

I think I'll take a little nap until my own good neighbor comes to lend *me* a hand!

SERVING THE DESERVING

ALL ABOUT **HELPING OTHERS**

Tagalong and I walked nearly two miles before that downpour hit. Jogging home in the rain sure refreshes the soul—and muddies the feet.

Ew! Look at this! My feet are filthy! I could start a vegetable garden here!

I'd better put this towel to good use if I want to keep the kitchen floor clean.

This towel reminds me of a story that took place in Jesus' day.

In Bible times, people walked just about everywhere. And they wore sandals, which meant their little piggies got pretty dirty. This little piggy stomped in puddles. This little piggy splashed in mud. And this little piggy squished into a camel pie! Gross!

No wonder people handed visitors a basin of water and a towel to clean their TOOTSIES at the door. Often a servant scrub-a-dubbed guests' feet before they came inside.

One day, the disciples headed to a dinner party at Jesus' house. "Come on, you slowpokes," Peter said to the other disciples.

Peter jogged ahead. "Jesus has something important to tell us," he called over his shoulder, "and I don't want to miss it."

"Peter! Really!" John replied. "If it's that important, Jesus will wait until we get there to say it."

Then Peter spied the house where Jesus was staying. "Hey! Last one there does the **dishes**," he yelled, breaking into a full run.

Jesus opened the door. "Wow! You're early!" He said. "Please come in and sit down."

"But our feet are dirty," Peter pointed out.

"Never mind about that now," Jesus replied. "Just come in."

The disciples sat around a **BANQUET** table heaped with fruit salad, lamb burgers, and goat milk shakes—the works! Mmmm.

The disciples chatted about the hottest new oxcarts while they ate. Then, saying He'd be right back, Jesus left the room.

The water in the basin sloshed as Jesus carried it into the room. He had wrapped a clean towel around His waist.

"John!" said Jesus. "Scoot around in your chair so I can wash your feet."

"Well, um, okay—w-whatever You say," John stammered.

Once John's feet were clean, Jesus turned to James. "You're next," Jesus said.

Splash! Scrub! Pat-pat-pat! James wiggled his spotless toes.

"Peter?" Jesus said. "Your feet, please!"

"What? No way are You washing my feet! I—You—we—that is—" Peter sputtered.

Jesus smiled. "It's okay, Peter. You don't understand now, but you will later. May I have your feet?"

Peter pounded the table with his fist. "**NO!**" he thundered. "You will never wash my feet. You are our King, not our servant."

"If I don't wash your feet, then you are not one of My people," said Jesus.

Peter shoved himself away from the table. "Well, in *that* case, give me a **whole** bath!" he cried.

Jesus smiled. "Just a foot bath will do," He said.

Peter stuck out his feet. "Sorry about that camel pie," he muttered. "We were racing and . . . well . . ."

After Jesus had washed everyone's feet, He said, "Today I became your SERVANT. Every good leader must serve others—showing kindness to everyone, regardless of who they are." He looked at Peter and grinned. "Or what they have on their feet."

Then Jesus told His disciples, "Follow My example. Be thoughtful and kind to everyone."

Jesus wants us to love others just like we love ourselves. And serving others shows them we love them—just like Jesus loved His disciples, and like He L♥VES us.

Well, my feet are clean! And to show Tagalong how much I love her, I'll wash hers next. Hey! Tagalong, where are you going? Come back, girl! Come here and let me wash your feet!

Jesus & the Little Children

JUST THE WAY YOU ARE

ALL ABOUT **HELPING OTHERS**

I've been looking for a **new** pair of sandals. But these hardly look new. They've got holes so big that my toes are leaking out. Whoever walked around in these babies probably wore out their feet, too.

Jesus walked all the time—just to help people. His sandals probably looked something like these. But that didn't stop Him. One grumpy guy tried to stop Him once, and, boy, did he learn a lesson!

One day, Jesus and His buddies hiked through Judea. They taught the people there to spread the Good News about God.

Everyone seemed to get into the spirit of things. Well, everyone except a grumpy guy named **MELViN.** He didn't like crowds.

"Oh," moaned Melvin, "swarms of people are rushing this way. Come on, Jesus. Let's sneak down another path."

"There He is!" a mom yelled, toting her two children.

As the mob rushed over, the grumpy guy threw himself between Jesus and the crowd, shouting, "Go away."

But the determined parents ignored him, pleading: "Jesus, please bless my child." "Jesus, can You heal my son's wart?" "Lord, please fix my daughter's voice. She can't sing a note."

Melvin shouted, "Get back! Take every wart, every vocal cord, every wet little face home! Jesus is too busy for your germy rug rats."

Calmly, Jesus said, "Let all the kids come to Me."
Jesus opened His arms and hugged all the children.
"Hello, Rachael," Jesus said. He brushed His hand across her little head. "Good to see you, Hannah and Roberto."
Something tickled Jesus' toes. Was it a bug? He looked down and discovered a little girl playing with His sandals.
"Would you like to try on My sandals, Ruthie?"
The child BEAMED as she pulled on sandals that were way too big.

"Jesus, shouldn't we be doing something more important?" asked the grumpy guy. "Don't we have hungry people to heal and sick people to feed . . . or something like that?"

"My dear Melvin," said Jesus kindly, "I also love to spend time with little **children,** like these."

Jesus gathered everyone around and spoke softly, as if He were sharing a big secret.

"God's kingdom belongs to children like these. No one can go to heaven without becoming like children."

The grumpy guy's eyes filled with tears, and his lower lip began to droop and wiggle.

"Y-You're saying I-I can't go to heaven if I'm not a little boy?" Melvin whined.

"That's not what I meant," answered Jesus.

"Children have the qualities God loves most," Jesus explained. "They trust Him. They are open with their feelings. They have faith in others. In these ways, we should never stop being like children. And we should always stop to help children in need."

Grumpy guy wiped away a *tear.*

"I'm sorry for keeping these little ones away," he said. "Even though they have wet faces."

Jesus smiled. "Your face is pretty wet too, buddy." And Melvin's grumpiness slipped away.

Clasping hands, everyone formed a CIRCLE around Jesus and Melvin and began to sing:

Jesus loves the little children,
All the children of the world.
Any color, dark or light,
They are precious in His sight.
Jesus loves the little children of the world.
                                    —Adapted by Mrs. Dan Whitaker

Melvin learned one of the best lessons that day. He learned how important it is to help all people! No matter what they look like, where they live, or how young they are.

Jesus loves everyone! And we should, too.

So take a good look at the people around you, and do something right **NOW** to help someone else. A good deed shows how much we care and reminds people how much Jesus loves us all!